No way!

Today was a
Making-Everyone-Better
day!

So Dylan dashed into
his kennel, and found . . .

. . . his doctor's kit!

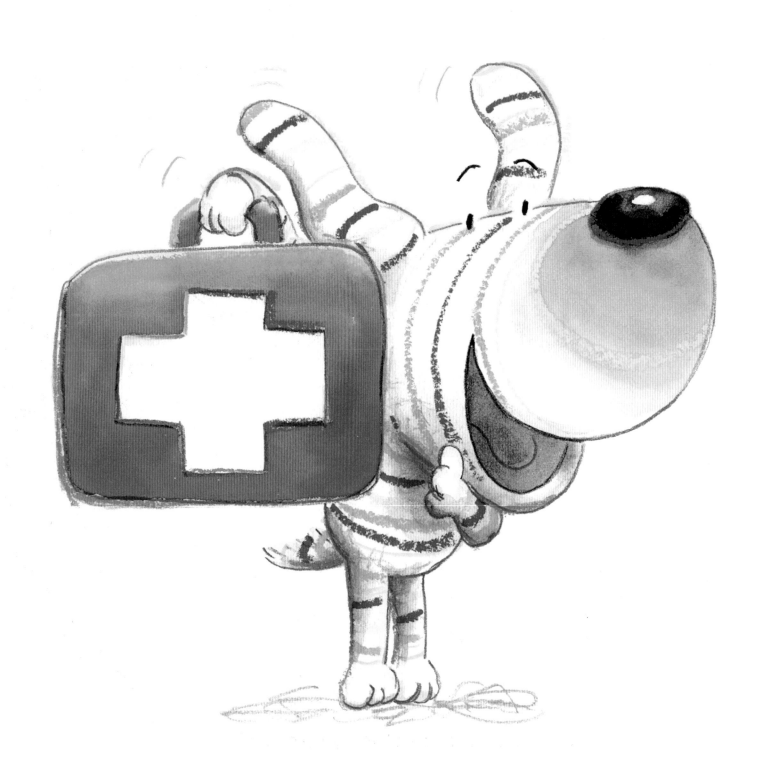

DYLAN
THE DOCTOR

Hello, I'm Dotty Bug.
Let's join in with
the story!

ALISON
GREEN
BOOKS

When it's a sunny day,
Dylan's ready to play.

But what sort of day was it today?
A quiet, stay-at-home day?

What do YOU like to play?

Was everything there?

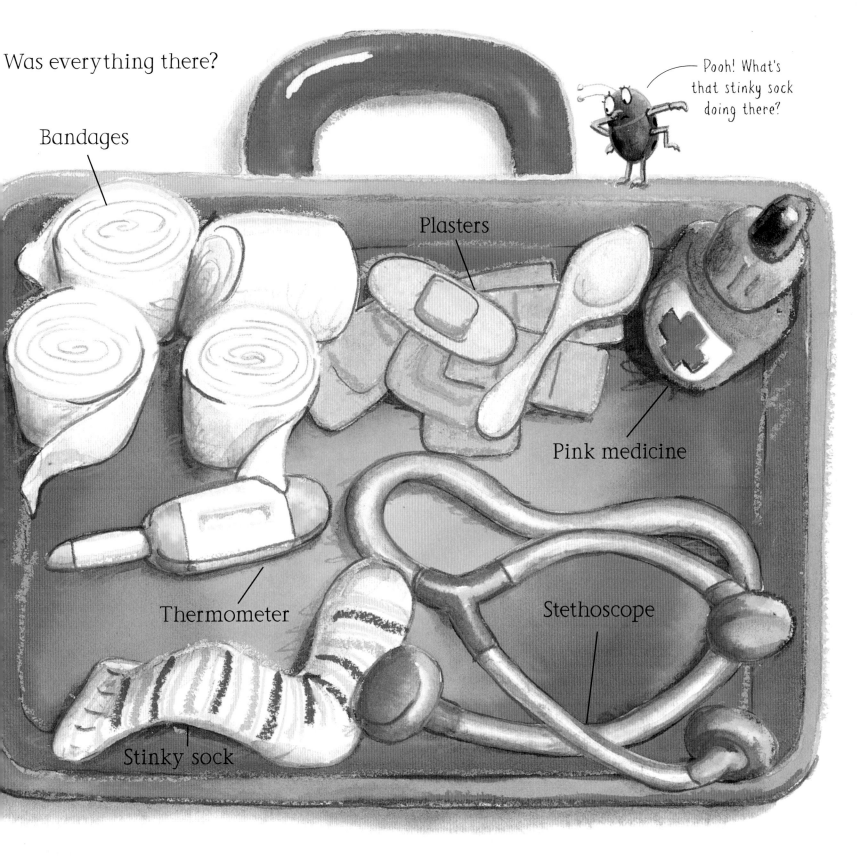

Bandages

Plasters

Pooh! What's that stinky sock doing there?

Pink medicine

Thermometer

Stethoscope

Stinky sock

Now, who needs Doctor Dylan's help?

Doctor Dylan zoomed down the path.

"Nee-naw, nee-naw, nee-naw!
Doctor Dylan on the way!"

Suddenly, he heard a cry.

Can YOU go
nee-naw, too?

It was Purple Puss.

"What's the matter, Purple Puss?"

"I've hurt my head, Doctor.
And my shoulders, knees and toes."

"Oh, no!" said Doctor Dylan.

"You've got Head-shoulders-knees-and-toes-itis."

He bandaged her up right away.

"Thank you, Doctor,"
said Purple Puss. "That's much better."

Doctor Dylan set off again.

"Nee-naw, nee-naw, nee-naw!
Doctor Dylan on the way!"

Suddenly, he heard a noise.

Flip-flap!
Flippety
flap!

What's that
funny noise?

It was Jolly Otter!

"What's the matter, Jolly Otter?"

"My tail feels too flappy!"

"Oh, no!" said Doctor Dylan.

"You've got Floppy-Wobble Fever."

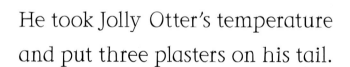

He took Jolly Otter's temperature
and put three plasters on his tail.

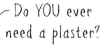

Do YOU ever
need a plaster?

"Thank you, Doctor!" said Jolly Otter.

"I'm feeling less flappy already."

Doctor Dylan was just about to set off
again when Purple Puss came running.
"Doctor! Quick! It's Titchy Chick! And it's an
EMERGENCY!"

EMERGENCY!"

Titchy Chick
didn't look very well.
"What's the matter,
Titchy Chick?"

Ooh, dear!

"Cheep!" said Titchy Chick,
but it was a very un-chirpy cheep.
"She needs to go to my hospital,
right away," said Doctor Dylan.

So they all made an
extra-loud ambulance noise:

"Nee-naw, nee-naw, nee-naw!"

and they rushed Titchy Chick
back to Dylan's kennel.

Have YOU ever been
in a hospital?

"What she needs," said Doctor Dylan,
"is lots of fuss."

So he plumped up a pillow,
and tucked her up with a blanket,
and gave her lots of pink medicine
and made a big fuss of her.

Titchy Chick was soon feeling much better.

That looks comfy.

When the other two saw Titchy Chick
getting so much fuss, they decided
that **they** felt a bit poorly, too.
"We need lots of fuss as well,
Doctor Dylan!" they said.

Do YOU like lots
of fuss, too?

So now Doctor Dylan had to look after everyone.

He plumped up everyone's pillows,
and gave everyone blankets,

and listened to everyone's chest,
and gave everyone pink medicine.

Then Jolly Otter needed a drink,
so Doctor Dylan gave him some juice.

And Purple Puss was hungry,
so Doctor Dylan brought her
some marshmallows.

That's pretty.

And Titchy Chick needed even
more fuss, so Doctor Dylan
made her a Get-Well-Soon card
(with glitter) to cheer her up.

Then he sang everyone a song,
and did them a dance,

and read them all a story.

At long last, Doctor Dylan said . . .

"I'm tired!

I need someone to make a fuss of me!"

"Oh, no!" said the others.
"Who's going to make a fuss of Doctor Dylan?"

Poor Doctor Dylan!

"We all are!"

said Doctor Purple Puss,
Doctor Titchy Chick
and Nurse Jolly Otter.

Do YOU like looking
after people?

And they made the biggest
fuss of him ever.

For Dylan,

and a big thank you to the
hugely creative Alison and Zoë

First published in the UK in 2016 by
Alison Green Books
An imprint of Scholastic Children's Books
Euston House, 24 Eversholt Street
London NW1 1DB
A division of Scholastic Ltd
www.scholastic.co.uk
London – New York – Toronto – Sydney – Auckland
Mexico City – New Delhi – Hong Kong

HB ISBN: 978 1 407166 25 4
PB ISBN: 978 1 407166 26 1

Printed in Malaysia

9 8 7 6 5 4 3 2 1

The moral rights of Guy Parker-Rees have been asserted.

Papers used by Scholastic Children's Books are made
from wood grown in sustainable forests.